Jesus Calms the Storm

Matthew 8:23-27
and Mark 4:35-41
for the beginning reader

Written by
Rosalie M. Gangwer

Illustrated by
Kathryn Mitter

St. Paul Books & Media

Library of Congress Catalog Card Number 93-17472

Gangwer, Rosalie M.
    Jesus Calms the Storm: Matthew 8:23-27 and Mark 4:35-41 for the beginning reader / written by Rosalie M. Gangwer: illustrated by Kathryn Mitter.
    p.   cm.
    Summary: A simple retelling, using only nineteen words, of the Bible story in which Jesus saves his friends by calming the wind and sea.

ISBN 0-8198-3955-8

    1. Stilling of the storm (Miracle)—Juvenile literature. 2. Jesus Christ—Miracles—Juvenile literature. [1. Stilling of the storm (Miracle) 2. Jesus Christ—Miracles. 3. Bible stories—N.T.]
    I. Mitter, Kathy. ill. II. Title.
    BT367.S74G26   1993
    226.7'09505 dc20

Printed and published in the U.S.A. by St. Paul Books & Media, 50 St. Paul's Avenue, Boston, MA 02130.

St. Paul Books & Media is the publishing house of the Daughters of St. Paul, an international congregation of women religious serving the Church with the communications media.

1 2 3 4 5 6 7 8 9   99 98 97 96 95 94 93

WORD LIST

(19 words)

see	oh
the	help
man	wind
is	away
Jesus	be
boat	still
go	makes
in	good
on	God
water	

See, see.
See the man.

See the man.
The man is Jesus.

See Jesus.
See the boat.

Go, go.
Go in the boat.

See the boat.
See the boat go on the water.

Oh, oh!
Oh, help!

See the water.
The water is still.

Jesus makes the water still.

Oh, oh.
Jesus is good.

Jesus makes the wind go away.
Jesus makes the water still.
Jesus is good.
Jesus is God.

Dear Parents/Teachers,

With a vocabulary of nineteen words, *Jesus Calms the Storm* has been designed to give the beginning reader a story about Jesus' power and goodness.

You can call attention to the fact that the men in the boat were afraid until Jesus brought the storm to an end. Most children can remember times when they were afraid. Explain that Jesus promised to be with us always. Awareness of Jesus' presence and goodness will help your child build faith in God and deal with fearful situations.

When your child is familiar with this book, you might like to read him or her the original account from the Bible (Matthew 8:23-27 or Mark 4:35-41).

If you share your own faith experience of how awareness of God's presence has helped calm the storms in your life, that will be a tremendous example for your child.

St. Paul Book & Media Centers

Visit, write or call your nearest St. Paul Book & Media Center nearest you:

ALASKA
750 West 5th Ave., Anchorage, AK
  99501 907-272-8183.

CALIFORNIA
3908 Sepulveda Blvd., Culver City, CA
  90230 310-397-8676.
1570 Fifth Ave. (at Cedar Street), San
  Diego, CA 92101 619-232-1442;
  619-232-1443.
46 Geary Street, San Francisco, CA
  94108 415-781-5180.

FLORIDA
145 S.W. 107th Ave., Miami, FL 33174
  305-559-6715; 305-559-6716.

HAWAII
1143 Bishop Street, Honolulu, HI 96813
  808-521-2731.

ILLINOIS
172 North Michigan Ave., Chicago, IL
  60601 312-346-4228; 312-346-3240.

LOUISIANA
4403 Veterans Memorial Blvd., Metairie,
  LA 70006 504-887-7631; 504-887-
  0113.

MASSACHUSETTS
50 St. Paul's Ave., Jamaica Plain,
  Boston, MA 02130 617-522-8911.
Rte. 1, 885 Providence Hwy., Dedham,
  MA 02026 617-326-5385.

MISSOURI
9804 Watson Rd., St. Louis, MO 63126
  314-965-3512; 314-965-3571.

NEW JERSEY
561 U.S. Route 1, Wick Plaza, Edison,
  NJ 08817 908-572-1200.

NEW YORK
150 East 52nd Street, New York, NY
  10022 212-754-1110.
78 Fort Place, Staten Island, NY 10301
  718-447-5071; 718-447-5086.

OHIO
2105 Ontario Street (at Prospect Ave.),
  Cleveland, OH 44115 216-621-9427.

PENNSYLVANIA
214 W. DeKalb Pike, King of Prussia, PA
  19406 215-337-1882; 215-337-2077.

SOUTH CAROLINA
243 King Street, Charleston, SC 29401
  803-577-0175.

TEXAS
114 Main Plaza, San Antonio, TX 78205
  210-224-8101.

VIRGINIA
1025 King Street, Alexandria, VA 22314
  703-549-3806.

CANADA
3022 Dufferin Street, Toronto, Ontario,
  Canada M6B 3T5 416-781-9131.